Scarlatti's Cat

For Chebbie and Ellie. And Stanley.
—N.L.

To my brother Joe, who makes the
most magical form of communication
there is in life—music.
—C.B.

Text copyright © 2014 by Nathaniel Lachenmeyer
Illustrations copyright © 2014 by Carlyn Beccia

Carolrhoda Books
A division of Lerner Publishing Group, Inc.
241 First Avenue North
Minneapolis, MN 55401 U.S.A.

For reading levels and more information, look up this title at
www.lernerbooks.com.

The paintings of Louis-Michel van Loo are used courtesy of
Wikimedia Commons.

Main body text set in Athenaeum Std 16/22.
Typeface provided by Monotype Typography.

Library of Congress Cataloging-in-Publication Data

Lachenmeyer, Nathaniel, 1969–
    Scarlatti's cat / Nathaniel Lachenmeyer ; illustrations by Carlyn
  Beccia.
        p.   cm
    Summary: Reveals how Pulcinella, a cat, contributed to one
  of the most popular symphonies written by eighteenth-century
  composer Domenico Scarlatti, and the consequences for the
  pampered pet.
    ISBN 978–0–7613–5472–7 (lib. bdg. : alk. paper)
    ISBN 978–1–4677–2401–2 (eBook)
    [1. Composers—Fiction. 2. Cats—Fiction. 3. Scarlatti, Domenico,
  1685–1757—Fiction.] I. Beccia, Carlyn, illustrator. II. Title.
  PZ7.L1335Scd 2014
  [E]—dc23   2013018648

Manufactured in the United States of America
1 – DP – 12/31/13

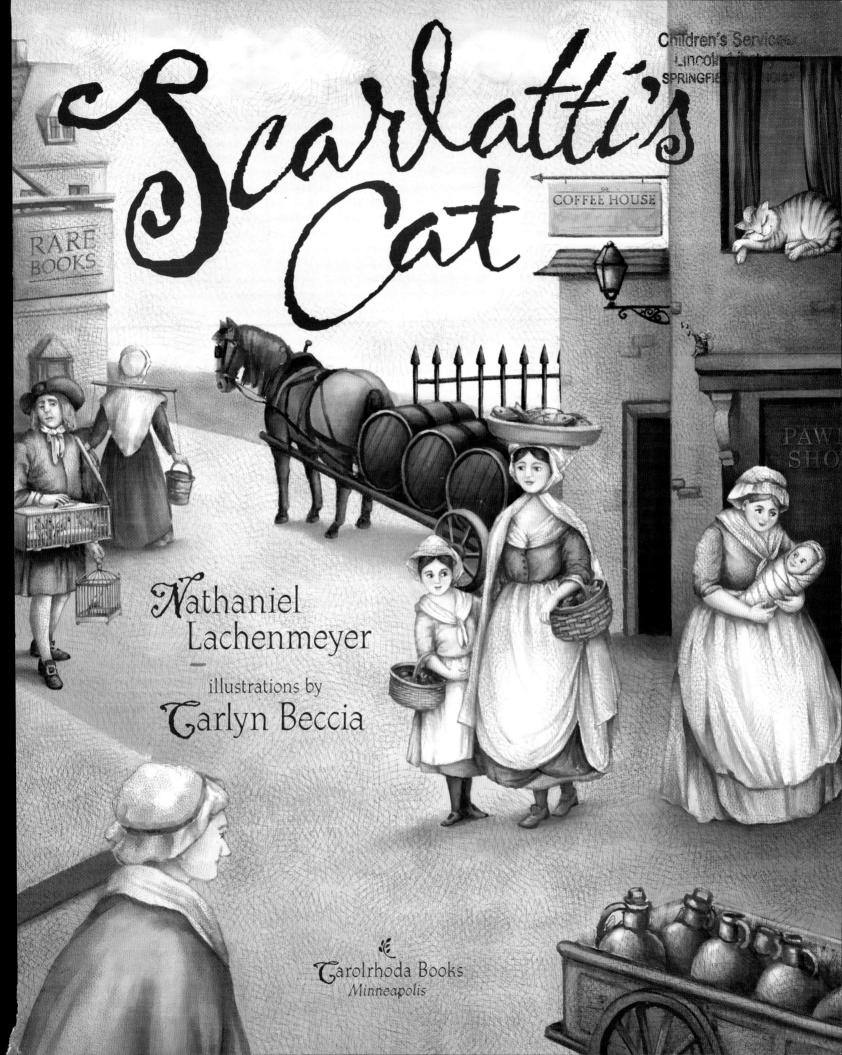

Scarlatti's Cat

Nathaniel Lachenmeyer

illustrations by Carlyn Beccia

Carolrhoda Books
Minneapolis

Scarlatti was a great Italian composer who lived a long time ago. So was his cat, Pulcinella, although no one knew it. Scarlatti sat all day long at his harpsichord, composing sonatas. Pulcinella usually sat by the window, basking in the sun.

Pulcinella liked basking in the sun. She liked listening to Scarlatti play. But what she wanted to do, more than anything, was compose. When she closed her eyes, she heard beautiful music that was all her own.

Every night Pulcinella dreamed about playing her music on the harpsichord.

Every morning Pulcinella stared longingly at the keys. But Scarlatti had one strict house rule: no one was ever allowed to touch his favorite instrument.

So Pulcinella kept her music to herself.

As Scarlatti's fame grew, he traveled across Europe. Everywhere he went, Pulcinella went too. She met some of the greatest composers of the day. Her favorite was George Frideric Handel, even though she thought he had very poor taste in pets.

Eventually, Scarlatti settled in the beautiful
city of Madrid, where he gave the Queen of
Spain music lessons. Pulcinella was treated
like a queen too. From time to time, she
still dreamed of playing the harpsichord,
but not as often as she used to.

If not for the arrival of an unexpected visitor, the world might never have discovered the music Pulcinella heard when she closed her eyes. Scarlatti did not notice the tiny creature tiptoeing across the floor.

ET PULCHRITUDINE

Pulcinella did.

Pulcinella chased the mouse up and down and around the room. When Scarlatti tried to shoo her away, she jumped on top of the harpsichord—

and landed on the keys.

The moment Pulcinella's paws touched the keys, she forgot all about the mouse. The music she heard when she closed her eyes came back to her like a sudden flash of sunlight. She knew this was her chance to live out her dreams. She began to walk daintily up and down the keys.

Scarlatti started to push her off, but then he heard the melody she was playing. He was amazed. It was as beautiful as anything he had ever written.

He grabbed his quill
and copied down the
notes as she played.

The next morning, Scarlatti carried
Pulcinella over to the harpsichord.
He wondered, would she play the
same sonata? Would she play at all?

As soon as her paws touched
the keys, she began to play a
new melody—the most perfect
melody he had ever heard.

Scarlatti reached for his quill. Then he stopped. "No! No! This won't do," he said to himself. "If anyone finds out that a cat can compose like this, what will become of Bach? What will become of Handel? What will become of ME?"

Scarlatti knew that he had no choice. He had to give Pulcinella away—and to someone who did not own a harpsichord.

Scarlatti could not bring himself to throw away Pulcinella's sonata. It was lovely, and it reminded him of her. Scarlatti gave Pulcinella as much credit as he could for the composition. He told people that he wrote it after listening to her walk across his harpsichord. To this day, the sonata is known as "The Cat's Fugue," in honor of Scarlatti's cat.

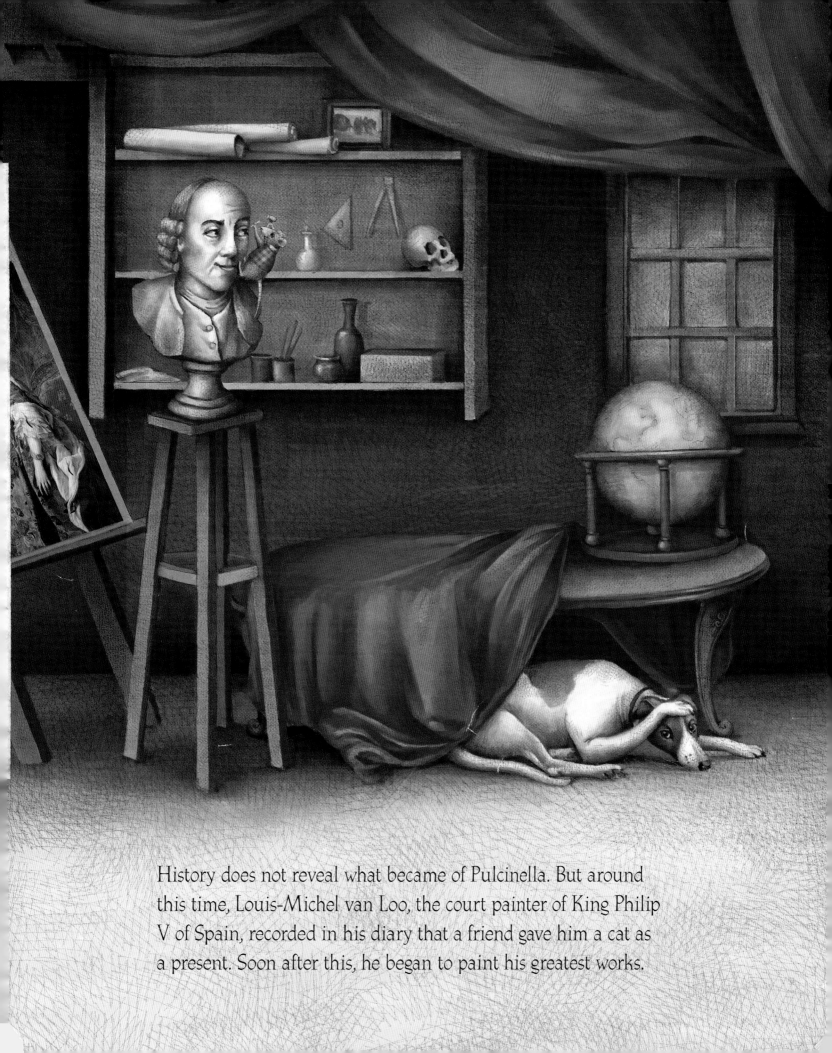

History does not reveal what became of Pulcinella. But around this time, Louis-Michel van Loo, the court painter of King Philip V of Spain, recorded in his diary that a friend gave him a cat as a present. Soon after this, he began to paint his greatest works.

Author's Note

The great Italian composer Domenico Scarlatti (1685–1757) is best remembered today for his sonatas. One of his most famous compositions is the Sonata in G Minor, popularly known as "The Cat's Fugue." According to legend, the distinctive melody of "The Cat's Fugue" was inspired by the notes Scarlatti's cat, Pulcinella, played when she walked up and down the keys of his harpsichord.